COUSIN JOHN IS COMING!

=AAAAA AHHH=

by Elise Broach • pictures by Nate Lilly

 DIAL BOOKS FOR YOUNG READERS

For "The Cousins"—
Sophie, Julia, and Elliot Broach, and Ellen, Jane, and Margaret Urheim—
who are not the least bit like Cousin John, but still the source of plenty of mischief and fun
—E.B.

To my parents, Paul and Anitra Lilly
—N.L.

DIAL BOOKS FOR YOUNG READERS
A division of Penguin Young Readers Group
Published by The Penguin Group
Penguin Group (USA) Inc., 375 Hudson Street, New York, NY 10014, U.S.A.
Penguin Group (Canada), 90 Eglinton Avenue East, Suite 700, Toronto, Ontario, Canada M4P 2Y3
(a division of Pearson Penguin Canada Inc.)
Penguin Books Ltd, 80 Strand, London WC2R 0RL, England.
Penguin Ireland, 25 St. Stephen's Green, Dublin 2, Ireland (a division of Penguin Books Ltd)
Penguin Books India Pvt Ltd, 11 Community Centre, Panchsheel Park, New Delhi - 110 017, India.
Penguin Group (NZ), Cnr Airborne and Rosedale Roads, Albany, Auckland, New Zealand
(a division of Pearson New Zealand Ltd).
Penguin Books (South Africa) (Pty) Ltd, 24 Sturdee Avenue, Rosebank, Johannesburg 2196, South Africa.
Penguin Books Ltd, Registered Offices: 80 Strand, London WC2R 0RL, England.

Text copyright © 2006 by Elise Broach
Pictures copyright © 2006 by Nate Lilly
The publisher does not have any control over and does not assume any responsibility
for author or third-party websites or their content.
Designed by Peonia Vázquez-D'Amico
Text set in Equipoize Sans-Bold
The art was created using pencil and digital color.

Library of Congress Cataloging-in-Publication Data
Broach, Elise.
Cousin John is coming! / by Elise Broach ; pictures by Nate Lilly.
p. cm.
Summary: After learning that the cousin he dislikes is coming for a visit,
a boy imagines what horrible things might happen to him.
ISBN 0-8037-3013-6
[1. Cousins—Fiction.] I. Lilly, Nate, ill. II. Title.
PZ7.B78083Co 2006
[E]—dc22   2004019406

Manufactured in China on acid-free paper
10 9 8 7 6 5 4 3 2 1

Ben, sweetheart, I have a very special surprise for you . . .

Cousin John is coming to spend
the weekend with us!

Isn't that exciting? His parents will drop him off Saturday morning.

You and Cousin John can play the games you always play,
like cowboys . . .

and superheroes . . .

and magicians.

It's just wonderful the way you two get along.

But no playing in the basement this time, Ben. Remember how that door sometimes sticks.

Oh, I forgot to tell you! Cousin John is going to bring a
pirate set that he got for his birthday. I know he'll share it
with you.

But you'll have to remember not to take him up in the tree house. He didn't like that for some reason.

We'll have to get your room ready. It will be so fun for you to have a sleepover. And you always go to bed so nicely! You never stay up too late talking.

And, sweetheart, for the whole weekend, we'll do just what you boys want to do. We'll make popcorn and watch movies . . .

And go to the playground . . .

You two are so good at entertaining yourselves!

We could even plan a special outing. Remember how we went to the carnival? Of course we'll have to make sure Cousin John doesn't wander off. We almost left him behind last time!

But you boys are older now. I'm sure that won't be a problem.
There are so many fun things we can do. We can go to the
beach . . .

and even the aquarium . . .

Oh, you boys will have such a great time together. And here's the best part: There's a good chance that Cousin John can stay all week!

Except, there's just one thing . . .

Cousin John got badly scratched by a cat a few months ago, and he's developed an allergy.

A terrible allergy. His face swells up like a balloon, his eyes
water, and he can't stop sneezing.

So we'll have to be careful to keep the kitty away from him.

When you're playing in your room . . .

And especially when you're eating . . .

Or at night, when you go to sleep . . .

I mean it, Ben. If we're not careful to keep the kitty away from Cousin John, he'll be perfectly miserable.

So miserable, he probably won't be able to stay with us. Do you understand?

Oh, Ben, isn't that nice!
I knew you'd be excited.